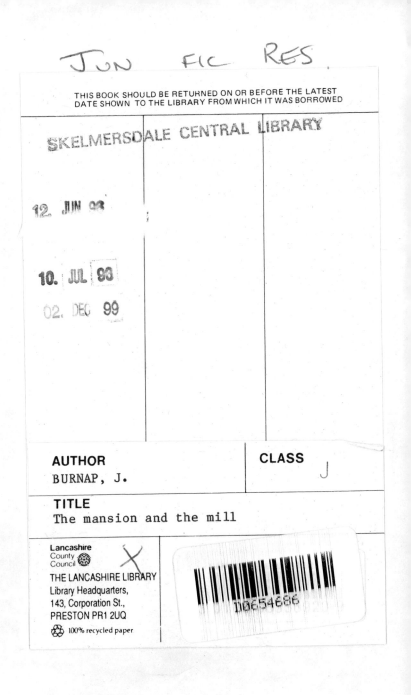

JUN FIC RES.

AUTHOR
BURNAP, J.

CLASS
J

TITLE
The mansion and the mill

THE MANSION AND THE MILL

By Jennifer Burnap

Illustrated by Edward Blake

(For George and Harriet)

ANGLIA *young* BOOKS

First published in 1994
by Anglia Young Books
Durhams Farmhouse
Ickleton
Saffron Walden, Essex CB10 1SR

Illustrations by Edward Blake

British Library Cataloguing-in-Publication Data

A catalogue record for this book is available from the
British Library

ISBN 1 871173 39 6

063369239

Typeset in Palatino and printed in Great Britain by
Redwood Books, Trowbridge, Wilts

CHAPTER ONE

The Family

It was nearly half past five by the time Polly reached home.

A bitter north wind had chased her all the way down Notley Street from the mill. It had almost whipped the old grey shawl from her head as she rounded the corner and came to a halt in front of the double gates into Pa's yard.

The gates were firmly shut. She was the first one home, as always.

Her icy fingers groped behind the loose brick to the left of the gate post and grasped the key. Then, holding the shawl tight about her, she battled once more round into Notley Street and let herself in at the door of Number 135.

Fumbling in the dark she skirted the old oak table and reached up to the mantle for the candlestick and matches.

The welcome glow of the candle flame lit up her pinched, cold face.

She warmed her hands for a moment before light-

ing the oil lamp. Now she could see all of their living room: the table and plain oak chairs, and the rockers on either side of the fire place. In a curtained alcove in one corner was Mam's and Pa's bed and on the other side of the room a simple oak dresser where Mam displayed her collection of modest china. The Queen's coronation mug took pride of place on the top shelf. Beside the dresser stood Daisy's cradle which she had grown out of now, but which Mam still kept 'just in case'. It was their best piece of furniture, for it had been hand-carved by Mam's own Pa when Joseph was born some eighteen years ago.

Still wrapped in her shawl, Polly took the iron

poker and rattled the ashes of last night's fire through the bottom of the fire box. She screwed up some paper and placed sticks on top and a few lumps of slag coal. Then, after putting a match to the paper, she pulled out the ashtray and tipped the contents into an old bucket by the back door.

While the flames licked through the kindling, she quickly ran around the little house checking the mouse traps; two from upstairs where she slept with Joseph, Grace and Davey, two from the living room and two from the scullery.

There was nearly always a mouse in each one.

One by one she pulled back the sprung wire and released the bodies into the flames of her new-made fire. Pa would reset the traps before they went to bed for, no matter how many they caught, there were always more grey furry bodies in the traps next time.

She was filling the kettle from the scullery pump when she heard the double gates clatter open and Belle and Moppet clip clopped into the yard. She had just enough time to make coffee and peel the potatoes. Pa would be at least twenty minutes taking the horses out of the wagon, hanging up the leathers and the heavy collars and then rubbing down and feeding the animals before he came in.

Before they had moved from Derbyshire, Pa had worked with the horses on a big farm, and Joseph with him, but last year had been a hard year on the land. Mr Cowan had told Pa that he would have to let him go. He had been fair enough, offering Pa the opportunity to start again in his own right by giving him the horses and the old wagon.

'Go to Lancashire, Bradshaw,' Mr Cowan had said. 'There's work for all the family there. Even the children. A good carter can't fail to find work hauling cotton or coal or such like.'

So they had packed all their belongings into the wagon, along with the hand carved cradle which had come in useful for Daisy who was born in June soon after they arrived in Coleybridge.

They had been lucky, for the mill owner, Sir John Taylor, had been hiring hands at the time. It was especially fortunate for Joseph who was mad about machinery and had worked as maintenance man on the farm. The mill had recently been converted to steam power after years of being dependent on the streams which coursed from the high moors.

Joseph assured the foreman that he could work any kind of machinery you cared to invent and, before long, he was assistant to the chief engineer. He was now earning more money than the best spinner in the mill, though his hours were longer because the engines which drove the spinning machines had to be producing a good head of steam by the time the spinners arrived at six o'clock.

Every evening, while Polly peeled the potatoes, she would amuse herself by remembering how beautiful and clean it had been living in the country, even in winter.

Coleybridge, with its rows of dingy back-to-back mill workers' houses, could not have been more different.

The only redeeming feature of Notley Street was

that the last house in the row had a stable yard and Pa had sufficient savings to pay the rent.

She had just finished the potatoes when Pa came in.

'Hello, In-between,' he said, chafing his cold hands together. 'The wind off the moor fair cuts you in half tonight. Have you got a mug of coffee for your old Pa?'

Polly brought him the steaming coffee. Pa peeled off his leather apron and unlaced his boots with the steel caulkers on the wooden soles.

'Where have you been today, Pa?' she said.

'Manchester. Took a load of calico down and brought back the usual load of raw stuff. What about you? Did you pay attention in that school-room of yours, In-between?'

Pa always called her 'In-between' because she was: in-between Joseph and Grace, the eldest, and Davey and Daisy, the youngest. It was his pet name for her and it made her feel a little bit special. That, and the schoolwork she was doing in the new schoolroom Sir John had set up for his mill workers' children. Pa set great store by book learning. He had learned to read and write at a tiny village school years ago and now, when he had to keep his own accounts for the carting business, he was able to write it all down in his beautiful copperplate hand. He had made sure that his children could do it, too. Education, Pa figured, could open doors for you. He wanted his children to do well in life and Polly's progress gave him great satisfaction, for she was a quick learner. Already she had mastered all the 'times tables' besides being able to read most of the few books in the schoolroom.

'We did the countries today, Pa,' she said brightly, bustling about laying the table.

'What countries?' He was allowing the cold water from the pump over the scullery sink to pour over his head and he was splashing it everywhere.

Polly jumped back out of the way.

'The countries of the Empire,' she said, reaching for the old coarse towel which hung on the back of the door. 'I'll tell you them as soon as I know them.'

'Good lass!' he said. 'Watch those potatoes now. Your Mam will be in soon.'

Grace was the next member of the family to arrive home. Polly heard the clatter of the clogs coming down the street and the 'Goodnights' called as the group of girls grew smaller at each front door.

Grace always came home to a lamp on the table and a fire in the hearth.

'By, that's cold!' she said, rushing in and slamming the door against the wind. 'I'm famished!'

Already Grace had lapsed into the way the other mill girls spoke. Being famished had nothing to do with hunger. Here in Lancashire it meant frozen. They all came home famished on winter evenings.

Grace was tall and slender with her mother's dark wavy hair and grey eyes. Already the young men were calling to take her out, but Grace would have none of it.

'I'm not interested in getting wed yet,' she would

say. 'I don't want to be tied to lots of children. I want to save my money first and have a good home when the time comes.'

Every week part of her wages was stored in a biscuit tin in her drawer in the tallboy upstairs. On pay days she divided it up: part for Mam, part for her simple wants, and part for her 'good home'. At weekends she would sit on the bed she shared with Polly and lovingly count it.

'A right miser you're getting, my lass,' Pa said, but he was proud for all that. Proud that his eldest daughter had 'her head screwed on right'.

Polly had no such luxury. All her wages, five shillings for a half timer piecing the threads when the yarn broke on the spinning machines, went into the family housekeeping.

By the time Grace had washed and added a little scrag end of mutton to the potatoes, Mam was home.

She never came in before twenty to seven for, though her shift ended at six as Grace's did, she still had to collect Davey who waited on the mill steps for her after his lessons. Then they went round to Mrs Wilkins for the baby.

Mam hated leaving Daisy with the childminder. The woman's house was dark and damp and she always had at least four children to care for. If one caught a chill they all caught a chill. If one had croop they all had croop.

As she came through the door that evening you could see she was cross. She had Davey by the ear, which was rough treatment indeed by Mam's standards.

'Get inside and get yourself washed,' she said harshly, adding a shove to his already twisted ear. She handed Daisy to Polly saying, 'That boy will be the death of me. Up at Shawcross's shop wasn't he? How many times have I told him I don't want him roaming around the streets in the dark? Made me late he has, and Daisy not too well either.'

'What's up with her, Mam?' Grace asked, cutting off thick slices of bread.

'I don't know. She seems sort of listless. I'm a bit worried. Mabel Duffy was saying that she heard that Doris Wilkins gives them laudanum to keep them quiet. I don't want her drugging a baby of mine.'

Grace poured her mother a cup of coffee.

'Here, Mam. Drink this. You're cold and tired. You don't want to set much store by what that woman says. She's a great one for telling an Irish yarn. They call it kissing the Blarney Stone and if anyone's kissed it Mabel Duffy has. I bet the whole of Manchester, not to mention Coleybridge, has heard of Mabel Duffy's stories.'

Soothed by her eldest daughter's advice and the warm coffee, Mam calmed down and when Davey emerged from the scullery clean and suitably peni-tent she managed to ask him quietly how many cops he had doffed that day.

'I lost count, Mam,' he said. 'Too many, I think.'

Like Polly, Davey was a half-timer and he spent the hours from six in the morning to one in the afternoon doing what was called 'doffing the cops', removing the full reels of yarn and placing them in a huge basket. All morning he ran from one machine to another replacing the full reels with new empty ones. In the afternoon he went to school like his sister but, as far as Davey was concerned, it was all very boring. He would much rather be playing marbles in the mill yard or hanging around Shawcross's shop in the hope of earning a penny for holding someone's horse. Once he had earned three pennies on a day when his charm had shone through his usual cheeky, up-to-no-good exterior.

'Mr Shawcross says there's goin' to be a war,' he suddenly announced.

'Don't talk rubbish, son. Get on with your supper,' Mam said, spooning mash and gravy into a very sleepy Daisy.

'A war!' scoffed Grace. 'Where does he get news like that from? War, indeed!'

'It's not rubbish,' Pa said. 'There's a lot of talk in the city. Not here, of course. In America.'

'Oh, there. It won't affect us then.'

Mam had lost her youngest brother in the Crimean War and she had never got over the shameful waste of sending soldiers so far away.

'Don't fret, Mother,' Pa said, mopping up the last of his gravy with a hunk of bread. 'America is a long way away, isn't it, Polly In-between? The other side of a big ocean, eh?'

'Yes, Pa. The Atlantic,' Polly agreed.

'There!' he said. 'I told you. Too far away to bother us.'

Polly, who was closer to him than the rest of the family, sensed there was a doubt in his voice. She wanted to ask why everyone was talking about it, but Pa busied himself with his plate and Polly knew the subject, for the moment anyway, was closed.

CHAPTER TWO

Florence

'What are you dreaming about, Polly Bradshaw?'

Miss Merryweather leaned over Polly's shoulder and flicked the page of the Bible which still lay open where it described Moses talking to God. 'Where had we got to, child?'

'I don't know,' Polly confessed.

A titter went round the class of raggle-taggle children. They were all the more amused because Polly was the clever one in the class. She was the one who usually knew the answers. She was the one who always had a clean pinafore on Mondays.

'Where are we, Agnes?' Miss Merryweather demanded.

Agnes, a plump unwholesome-looking girl who rarely got a chance to shine, answered immediately,

'Exodus, Chapter 34, Verse 29, Miss. Moses has the tablets with all the Lord's commandments on them, Miss.' She smirked virtuously in Polly's direction.

'Well done. I'm glad to see someone is paying attention this afternoon. Perhaps you'd like to continue with the reading now, Polly?'

Polly quickly turned to the correct page and she was just about to read when a man came into the room. He was dressed all in black with smart shining leggings over his boots. He doffed his cap politely as he entered.

'Beg pardon, Miss, but Sir John is outside in the

carriage with some books for your classroom. Would you care to send a couple of children outside to carry them in?'

Miss Merryweather, a lady of at least forty years of age, was instantly thrown into a twitter of activity.

'How kind! How very kind!' she said over and over again. 'Polly! You and Tom run and help this gentleman to bring in the books. And mind your manners!'

The two children followed the man out into the mill yard where Sir John's carriage stood with its finely groomed pony.

'Ah, here you are!' Sir John himself stepped down from the carriage.

He was very tall with slightly greying hair and the most handsome set of whiskers Polly had ever seen. He seemed to tower over them both and his size was made even greater by the voluminous cloak he wore.

'Pass down the books, Hambrook. This lad looks strong. You're a good strong lad, aren't you?

'Yes, sir,' said Tom.

About ten books of various sizes were loaded on top of one another in Tom's arms until he very nearly disappeared behind the pile.

Then four or five were passed down to Polly who was bending her head sideways to read the titles: The Holy Roman Empire, Wayside Flora and Fauna, A Child's Introduction to Science.

The pile began to wobble and the top one fell to the ground.

Embarrassed at her clumsiness Polly bent her knees and groped for the book while trying to balance the others. Sir John beat her to it.

'Squinting at the titles, eh, child?' he said placing the book back before she dropped any more.

'Yes, sir.' She tried to curtsey, but thought better of it.

'You're a good reader then?'

'Yes, sir.'

'What's your name, child?'

'Polly Bradshaw, sir.'

'Ah! You must be Bradshaw the carter's daughter?'

'Yes, sir. One of them.'

'And do all your father's children read well?'

'Yes, sir. But I'm the best.'

Sir John hooted with laughter just as Miss Merryweather came out into the yard to thank their benefactor for his generous gift.

'This pupil of yours does you credit, Ma'am,' he said.

Miss Merryweather cast an anxious glance at Polly.

'I trust she has been respectful, sir.'

'Of course, Miss Merryweather. What else should I expect from your charges?'

Blushing with pleasure, she dismissed Polly and her armful of books.

'She's a good student, that Polly Bradshaw?' Sir John asked as he shook the lady's hand and climbed back into the carriage.

'The best I have, sir, but lacking in modesty at times.'

'Well, I've brought her a few more books to fuel her eager mind, ma'am.'

Miss Merryweather uttered her grateful thanks and the carriage drove out of the mill gates.

. . . . .

It was Sunday and Polly was in the yard brushing Belle. She loved the horses. They were so large and powerful, yet so patient. They spent all of their lives trudging from Coleybridge to the city, or even to the docks at Liverpool. On such a journey they were often away several days at a time. Polly wondered if they missed the countryside like she did. Did they remember the haymaking, bringing in the harvest, or ploughing in winter? Sometimes she asked them as she groomed them but their only reply was to nuzzle her ear or flick her with their tails when she brushed their fetlocks.

This Sunday afternoon she had given them a special grooming because it had rained heavily the day before and they had come home caked with mud.

Suddenly Mam flung open the back door and called for Pa.

'Quickly!' she said. 'There's a messenger here from his Lordship. He has a note for you.'

'For me?' A frown creased Pa's forehead. He'd

been shovelling horse manure from the stable and he was embarrassed at being summoned to the door in his filthy clothes. When he returned to the yard he looked even more uncomfortable.

'What have you been up to, In-between?'

'Nothing, Pa. Why?'

'Sir John wants me to take you up to the Hall tomorrow afternoon.'

'But you'll be on the road, Pa.'

'That will have to wait. He wants you to meet his daughter Florence, who is the same age as you and rarely sees other girls. Why has he asked for you I wonder?'

Polly shrugged her shoulders. 'Perhaps because he met me last week. He asked me if I could read and I said I could.'

'Is that all you said?'

'I said I was good at it, Pa.'

He shook his head. 'What am I going to do with you, In-between? You are getting too big for your boots, my girl.'

Still shaking his head he went back to his shovelling wondering where this confidence of his middle daughter would lead them.

As they had been instructed Pa and Polly drove up Notley Street on Monday afternoon. They passed the mill with its three floors of looms and spinning machinery, its rows and rows of windows and tall smoking chimneys. Then they headed out of town where the grey rows of workers' houses gave way to smart villas with gardens, and finally out onto the edge of the moor.

Here stood Denbigh Hall, the home of Sir John Taylor and his family.

The wagon turned in at the imposing gateway and began the slow trek up a long driveway, through an avenue of tall beeches, and finally around a vast lawn in front of the house itself.

And what a house it was!

There seemed to be so many rooms that Polly wondered how one family could live in them all.

The house was built of mellowed red brick with black bricks inserted in patterns here and there. The windows were tall and some had coloured glass borders while others built into the roof had little green domes above them.

'It's like a palace, Pa!' Polly said. 'How can one family live in a house as big as that? I'd get lost in there.'

'Aye, lass. That you would.'

It was at times like this he wished he owned a smaller wagon and didn't need to take out both horses. A one-horse cart would look so much better for calling on the gentry. Perhaps one day he would have saved enough to buy one.

They didn't drive up to the grand front door, but turned left and went through an archway into a yard where the tradesmen's entrance was.

Here Pa tied the horses to a hitching post set in the centre of the yard beside a stone mounting block and a horse trough. Then he and Polly walked to the door and rang the bell.

They could hear the bell echoing through the passages of stone-slabbed floors and then the tap-tapping of a lady's heels approaching.

The door was opened by a severe-looking woman whose greying hair was scraped back into a bun. There wasn't a hair out of place. Not like Mam's wavy hair escaping from its pins on wash day, Polly thought.

The housekeeper stood at the door, all starched collar and cuffs and one raised eyebrow.

'Yes?' she demanded.

'Bradshaw, Ma'am,' said Pa. 'And my daughter Polly.'

He twisted his best cap into a roll, the only sign that he was at a loss to know what to say.

'Sir John asked to see me, Ma'am,' Polly said, by way of explanation.

'Indeed!' The other eyebrow shot up. Someone had obviously neglected to tell her.

'Wait here!' she snapped, and her heels click-clacked back along the passage. Polly slipped her hand into Pa's, as much to reassure him as herself.

When the woman returned she told Pa he could go and Sir John would send the child back later.

'Off you go then, In-between, and remember what I said about your boots.'

Polly reached up and kissed his cheek. She certainly didn't feel too big for her boots at this moment.

The housekeeper led her through long corridors and up stairs and across a hall where black and white tiles made the floor look like a giant chequers board. At every turn there were paintings and wonderful ornaments and the most incredibly grand furniture.

At last they reached a door at the rear of the house and here the housekeeper knocked and waited and then pushed Polly ahead of her into the room.

On a *chaise-longue* sat Sir John Taylor's wife, a lady of comfortable proportions with rich copper hair piled high on her head. She wore an elegant dress of fine green wool which complimented her colouring and her whole bearing was in direct contrast to Mrs Poole, her housekeeper.

'So this is Polly Bradshaw,' she said, rising and taking Polly's hand. 'My husband tells me that you are a clever young lady,' she said warmly.

'Not really,' stammered Polly, curtseying and re-membering what Pa had said not five minutes ago.

'Well Sir John thinks you will get on well with my daughter so let's go and find her shall we?'

Mrs Poole, somewhat dismayed to find her employer entertaining a common carter's daughter, went stiffly away.

Her Ladyship led Polly up the grand staircase to a room on the first floor which was a cross between a sitting-room and a schoolroom.

Here a girl of about Polly's own age sat at the table poring over a book with an elderly lady, who was struggling to teach the child something called French Verbs.

'Ah!' said her Ladyship. 'You two are busy I see. Now here is Polly who has come to spend the afternoon with you, my darling. Polly, this is my daughter Florence. I told her you were coming. Mademoiselle, I think you and I will leave these two young ladies to get to know one another.'

The French teacher closed her books and the two ladies left the room.

Florence looked at Polly. Polly looked at Florence. There was an uncomfortable silence.

Florence was a smaller version of her mother with the same copper curls and creamy complexion. Her dress was plain but made of the same fine cloth and her pinafore was crisply starched and trimmed with broderie anglaise lace and fine, hand-sewn tucks.

Polly, on the other hand, wore a grey calico dress

sewn by Mam and a plain pinafore. She was clean and tidy, but the only claim to luxury she wore was her best blue hair ribbon twined into her thick plait of fair hair.

'Father says you are the carter's daughter,' Florence finally said.

'Yes,' Polly replied lamely.

'He says you read well. Do you know French?'

'No.'

'What do you know?'

Polly resented this interrogation but she replied politely.

'Reading, Writing and Arithmetic, History, Geography, Sewing and the Bible, Miss.'

'Can you play any games?'

'Not many. I don't have time. I work at the mill all morning and do lessons in the afternoon. When I get home I have to help in the house.'

'Do all the children work?' Florence swung her legs from under the table and looked a little more interested.

'Most of them do. When they're old enough. What do you do?' Polly felt braver now.

'Nothing. Only lessons with Ma'amselle and drive out with Papa sometimes. Mama pushes me round the garden when the weather is warmer.'

'Pushes you?'

'In my chair.'

Only now did Polly notice that Florence had a damaged foot. It was encased in a specially made boot of soft leather and the sole was about five centimetres thick.

She immediately felt sorry for the girl.

Here she was, living in a palace, surrounded by fine furniture, dressed in the best clothing and driven everywhere in a shiny carriage with a grey pony and yet she had nothing. What good was luxury if you couldn't run or play like other children? She was a prisoner in her palace!

'Do you have any brothers or sisters?'

'Only a brother, but I don't see much of him. He's older than I and is away at school. Anyway, when he is at home he doesn't have time for me. Papa wants him to learn all about the mill. Would you like me to teach you to play chequers?'

Polly agreed and Florence limped to a sideboard and brought the chequers board and the black and white pieces.

For nearly an hour the girls played and at half past three a manservant brought them milk and little fancy cakes. When Florence's Mama looked in to see how they were getting on she was relieved to see how happy they were.

She stood behind Florence's chair and stroked her hair.

'Perhaps when the weather is warmer we can arrange an outing or two for you both. Papa will be so pleased to see that you are friends. He has been quite worried about you lately, my dear. Now I must go and see Cook about the dinner. Hambrook will take you home at half past four before it gets dark, Polly.'

Polly made a little curtsey. 'Thank you Ma'am.'

'Papa has been worried about a lot of things lately,' Florence said thoughtfully as her mother closed the door. 'It's all this talk of war, you know.'

'Davey – that's my little brother – he said something about that the other day, but our Mam thought he was talking rubbish as usual.'

'I don't think it's rubbish,' said Florence. 'It's something to do with America where most of our cotton comes from. If there's a war and we can't get the cotton Papa's mill won't be able to do any spinning and weaving. Do you know anything about America, Polly?'

'Not much,' Polly admitted. 'I know where it is, but that's all. Perhaps I'll ask Miss Merryweather tomorrow.'

'Will you tell me if you learn anything? I would so much like to surprise Papa. I sometimes think he despairs of my education for Francis knows so much more than I. He even learns Latin!'

'Latin!' exclaimed Polly. 'The Romans spoke Latin. I don't see why that should be so important. They're all dead!'

'Exactly,' agreed Florence, and the new friends laughed together.

CHAPTER THREE

Half Time

Polly rode home in style that afternoon, but she was very glad that it was dusk and no one was around to see her. Her friends would have thought she was getting a 'mite uppity', arriving home in a carriage.

She thanked Mr Hambrook kindly then fled round the side of the house to grope for the key in its usual hiding place.

By the time the family came home she was changed out of her Sunday best, the fire was lit, the potatoes on and the coffee hot on the hob.

Everything seemed normal except that little by little an unease was creeping into their lives.

This became even more noticeable when Joseph came home that evening.

He was very late and the family had all eaten.

Daisy, who still seemed pale and listless, had at last gone fretfully to sleep in the little cot at the foot of her parents' bed, behind the curtain.

Pa was painstakingly doing his accounts while

Mam and Grace sat mending. Davey was on the floor playing with a beetle in a matchbox and Polly was practising her spellings for tomorrow.

The bitter north wind was threatening to take the door off its hinges as Joseph came in.

'You're late, son,' Mam said as he unwound his scarf and hung it with his cap on the peg behind the door. 'Come to the fire, Joey. It's a wicked cold night. Where have you been?'

'Union meeting, Mam.'

'I thought as much. Trouble is it?'

'Could be, Mam. There's talk of laying some folk off if this war gets started. These mills depend on American cotton. Things could be bad for us if we can't get it.'

'There's always Indian cotton,' said Pa.

'Aye, but it's rubbish compared with what we have now. The staple is shorter for one thing and, besides, bringing it from India is a whole lot more expensive. It's such a long journey and journeys cost money.'

'I know where India is,' said Polly. 'The Queen is Empress of India. It's coloured pink on our map in the schoolroom, like all the other countries of the Empire.'

'Does that mean they have pink grass?' asked Davey, easing the beetle back into the box.

''Course not, stupid!' Polly said, giving him a playful shove. 'All the countries that belong to us are coloured pink. It's just so you know who governs them.'

'All right, Miss Clever Clogs,' Mam said, rolling up the sock she had just finished mending. 'You and Davey get to bed now.'

As they crept under the sheets and tucked their toes in their nightshirts, they could still hear the murmur of voices below talking about the war. Polly was even more determined to ask Miss Merryweather about it tomorrow.

'You awake still, Davey?' she whispered.

'What?'

'Did you notice how they were so busy talking about the war that no one asked me how I got on at the Hall today?'

'How did you get on?'

'Fine. Miss Florence is a very nice girl. She's crippled you know. Crippled and lonely. I think she liked me. I'm going again next Monday. Mr Hambrook will pick me up in the carriage. It's a beautiful house. Like a palace. You listening, Davey?'

Davey was fast asleep.

. . . . .

Polly was awake before the 'knocker up' came down Notley Street at half past five next morning. She laid in bed curled up beside Grace and watched the flicker of light from his lantern crossing their ceiling. Then there came the tap-tap of his long stick against the window and the clatter of his clogs moving on across the road to go up the other side of the street.

Mam was already up. She had cut two thick slices

of bread and cheese and wrapped them in a clean cloth for Pa to take on his journey down to Manchester and he had set off with the wagon ten minutes ago. Joseph too had gone and, by the time the workers reached the mill at six o'clock, the engine room would already be ticking over, well-oiled and gleaming.

Barely speaking to each other, the rest of the family drank their coffee then joined the throng of grey clad workers making their way through the dark wet streets to the mill.

Inside the mill was warm and dry but the noise of machinery was deafening. The oily smell that pervaded the lofty rooms would have been quite obnoxious to Florence had Sir John ever brought her there.

To Polly and Davey it was part of their everyday life, as it was for all the children of Coleybridge.

All morning Polly and her friends dived between the looms where their nimble fingers retrieved the broken threads and twisted and rejoined them. The younger ones, like Davey, replaced the reels.

At eight o'clock everyone stopped for a welcome break of bread and coffee or oatmeal porridge with a swirl of black treacle melting in it.

That morning as the women gathered at the end of the spinning room the talk was all of the possibility of half-time work.

Sir John Taylor was a generous employer. Not every mill owner provided his workers with hot porridge and afternoon schooling for the children, even if their teachers were maiden ladies with few qualifications, and their books donated by wealthier folk.

All this would matter little if their mill had no cotton. However good his Lordship was, everyone knew he could not run the mill without cotton.

At last their shift was over. The children ate a hot potato baked below in the engine room, then they filed into the schoolroom at the far end of the mill, away from the noise and the smell and the choking dust of the raw cotton.

All afternoon they worked away until finally Miss Merryweather dismissed them.

Now was the moment Polly had been waiting for. She helped clear away the slates and chalks and stood politely by the teacher's table.

'Yes, Polly?' Miss Merryweather peered up at the girl through her funny half spectacles.

'May I ask you something, please Miss?' Polly began hesitantly.

'Of course. What is it?'

'Everyone is talking about a war in America. Can you tell me why, please?'

Miss Merryweather searched along the book shelf and handed Polly a book called *Uncle Tom's Cabin*.

'This story will help you understand what is going on in America. It was written nine or ten years ago and it's all about slaves who work in the cotton fields. The States of the North want slavery to be stopped, but the States of the South want cheap labour to grow their cotton. It seems that the North and the South are prepared to fight for their beliefs, but if this happens we won't get any cotton and without cotton this mill, and many others, won't be able to keep going.'

'My Pa says there's always cotton from India.'

'That's true, Polly, but the quality is not as good and the staple, that is the fibres, are shorter, which means it won't make such fine cloth. And besides, it takes much longer to reach us. Come. Let me show you.'

Miss Merryweather took Polly over to the wall where was hung the large map of the world showing the countries of the Commonwealth and the British Empire.

'See how far the ships must sail. Across the Indian Ocean to the southern tip of Africa. Then northwards up the Atlantic side of that continent, and on past Portugal and France and then into the Irish Sea to Liverpool. That is a trip of three months or more. Of course it will be easier when the new Suez Canal is finished but that is some years away yet.'

'So Sir John will be worrying too?'

'Yes, I'm sure he will, for the price will be higher and we may be short of cotton for months. Who can tell? There are more than four million people in Britain who earn their living from cotton one way or another. Everyone has reason to fear this war. Even though it's not our battle and our men will not fight in it, there will be much suffering I'm afraid.'

'Thank you for showing me, Miss. I guess people

like my Pa will also be short of work if there is no cotton to carry?'

'Everyone, and I mean everyone, from the little children like your Davey to the shopkeepers who sell your Mam her groceries, even up to Sir John and all the merchants and mill owners. Only folk who have money saved will manage to survive reasonably.'

'My Pa has been saving for another cart,' Polly said thoughtfully. 'But perhaps there won't be anything to carry in it anyway.'

'Maybe not, dear.'

. . . . .

It was a very subdued girl who went home through the dark streets that afternoon.

She resolved to say nothing to the family but, after supper was cleared away, she sat herself at the table and began to read the book Miss Merryweather had given her.

It was an amazing story and one which explained many things about life as a slave and, as soon as she had finished it, she lent it to Florence to read.

It was the beginning of April and there was still a cold wind off the moor. Often the rain lashed the grimy mill town of Coleybridge with fierce slanting showers which Mam described as 'stair rods' even though stair rods were for folk who actually owned a stair carpet.

Nevertheless the dead winter grass on the hills gave way to a fresher green and the daffodils appeared in the gardens of the finer houses. There were acres of them in the park at Denbigh Hall, and on some Monday afternoons Polly and Florence were driven out to get some air, well wrapped in a fleecy rug.

The two girls were firm friends now and Polly was allowed to push Florence around the walled gardens and through the long greenhouses full of sweet-smelling carnations. To Polly, such beauty and tranquility seemed a million miles away from the troubles of Notley Street and the increasing fear of being out of work. On wet days they played cards or board games, but what they enjoyed most was to spend time in the vast kitchen with Mrs Dawkins.

Mrs Dawkins was plump and jolly. She was always dressed in a striped skirt and crisp white blouse and her voluminous apron was fresh starched every day. She had two kitchen maids and a scullery maid to help her and there was also an elderly man called a butler. He seemed to be in charge of all the household staff, though the housekeeper, Mrs Poole, and Mrs Dawkins were directly answerable to her Ladyship herself.

Polly never ceased to marvel at the wonderful kitchen with its shining copper pans, huge, black, polished range and enough china and glass to serve an army.

On a rack above the door hung twenty little bells each numbered to represent the rooms of the Hall. When a bell rang one of the servants hurried to answer the summons.

Sometimes the two girls would sample the newly

baked pastries or the huge bowl of fresh fruit salad and Mrs Dawkins would give them milk straight from the dairy.

As money got tighter for the mill workers, Mrs Dawkins would give Polly a bag of vegetables to take home.

'These are for your Mam and no questions asked, mind,' she'd say, then she'd tap her nose to indicate that it was a secret and bundle Polly into the carriage waiting at the back door.

In that month the war in America began in earnest and all through the summer and on into autumn the situation in town grew worse.

The mill was still managing to run on its stocks of cotton, but only on half time which meant half wages for most of the workers.

Polly didn't fully understand all that was going on but as she had shown such an interest in the American war Miss Merryweather told her how the Government of the Northern States had stopped the ships entering and leaving the Southern ports. This was called 'the blockade' and, in some places, huge rocks had been dropped in the water to prevent the passage of ships. Now no more cotton would get through.

With nothing to carry to and from the docks Pa had a hard time finding customers. One night he came home with a load of sacking left over from the cotton bales.

'Do you think you can sew us some sacks, girls?' he said.

'Sacks!' exploded Grace. 'We haven't come to wearing sacks yet, Pa.'

'They're not to wear, lass,' he said. 'Tomorrow I'm going to bag up the horse manure. Maybe I can sell it around the fine houses. It's the best fertilizer a garden can have.'

He sounded cheerful enough about his new enterprise but Polly knew there was desperation behind his smile and she wondered if he too dreamed of the countryside they had left behind and his cottage garden full of vegetables.

CHAPTER FOUR

Getting By

Christmas came and went very poorly that year for the Bradshaw family.

Joseph was the only one still earning reasonable money because the mill engines had to run for part of the day, but Mam and Grace only had half-time money and Davey and Polly stayed at home to look after Daisy. That way Mam no longer had to pay the child minder.

If there was anything good about being on half time it was that Daisy could be cared for at home. She was a pale sickly baby and seemed to catch every chill that was going around. Mam often had to boil a pan of water with tar in it so that the steam eased her breathing.

Pa managed to sell all the manure he could bag up, but now his greatest worry was actually feeding the horses.

One bleak January day the carriage picked Polly up as usual. Seeing Florence was the one bright spot in the week.

This Monday, however, even the Taylor family

were subdued and Florence was dressed in mourning.

'What has happened?' Polly asked as soon as they were alone in the sitting-room where Florence did her lessons with Mademoiselle.

'There has been a big mine disaster up at Newcastle upon Tyne. Papa's brother was one of the owners there.'

'Was?'

'He was killed, along with about two hundred others.'

What little Polly knew of mining, it seemed to be a very dangerous occupation, and certainly not one in which the owner himself went down the mine.

'Papa says he was doing an inspection. Uncle Thomas was rather like Papa. He was always checking on the welfare of his workers. He and the foreman were just going down in the cage when the shaft collapsed. Papa is very upset for he and Uncle Thomas were very close.'

'I'm sorry,' Polly said but it sounded dreadfully inadequate.

'What with this and poor Prince Albert dying just before Christmas, and the troubles at the mill, all the country seems to be in mourning.'

'My Pa is worried too,' Polly said. 'He's using more and more of his savings just to feed us and now he's short of fodder for the horses. The farmer where we used to live has offered Pa a cartload of hay, but what use is that when he has to pay money at the turnpike to get it?'

'Why does life have to be so beastly?' grumbled Florence. 'Here. Push me down to the kitchen and we'll sample Mrs Dawkin's plum tarts'.

Ramps had been fitted to most of the stairways in Denbigh Hall and this enabled Florence and her wheelchair to get to nearly all of the rooms. It was on one of their excursions around the house that they came upon Florence's brother Francis. He was home for the Christmas holidays and was due back at Rugby the following weekend.

He was tall and reddish haired like his mother, but he did not have the natural good manners or concern for people that his parents had. In fact he was quite rude about Polly.

'I cannot understand why Papa has entertained a carter's daughter in this house,' he said, loftily. 'My friends would be quite put out if I were to mention that my sister was hobnobbing with one of our workers.'

'Well, don't tell them,' Florence snapped back at him. 'If your friends spent more time studying and less in gossip about things they know nothing of they might be fit to run their family businesses one day.'

'Let me tell you, little sister, the fellows spend quite enough time on rubbish like Greek and Latin. They need a little relaxation from time to time.'

'I used to think that Latin was rubbish too, but Miss Merryweather says that it is the root of all European languages,' Polly said sharply.

'Good Lord! It thinks it's educated too, does it?'

'Don't be rude, Francis. Polly knows a lot of things

I bet you've never heard of, and she's my friend which is more than you are.'

'Spoiled brat!' Francis retorted and swaggered out of the room whacking his riding boots with his crop.

'I hate him!' Florence growled. 'He's always been jealous of me because Mama and Papa have to look after me more than him. He forgets that I'll never be able to do the things he does like going to parties and balls and things. He was very rude to you, Polly.'

'Don't worry about it,' Polly reassured her friend. 'I just hope he improves before he inherits your Papa's mill. If he behaves like that he'll have all the workers out on strike in no time.'

Florence's frown turned to laughter.

'Perhaps I'd better warn Papa of that,' she giggled. 'For when we get cotton again, eh?'

The poverty that the lack of cotton was causing became even more obvious to Polly when Mr Hambrook drove her home that January afternoon.

Next door at Number 133 a man was loading a bed, mattress, and an old chest of drawers onto a hand cart and Mrs Hemmings was standing clutching her apron to her mouth to stop her tears. Her two tiny children clung to her skirts, not understanding, while all along the street neighbours watched in sympathy and fear.

Polly leapt down from the carriage and ran in doors. It seemed very wrong to be coming home in style when Mrs Hemmings was selling her bed.

Polly put the bag of vegetables on the table.

'Mrs Hemmings is selling her bed, Mam,' she said.

'Aye. And it could be us next,' Mam replied as she divided the vegetables and sent Davey next door with half of them.

'Do you really think so, Mam?'

'Well, so far we're managing, but the money Pa saved for the new cart has all gone. Grace has been

good letting me have some of her savings but I hate taking it off the lass. It was for her own home one day. It might be months before she can save that much again. I tell you, Polly, there's times when I wonder where it will all end.'

'Mr Shawcross has a notice outside his shop, Mam. It says, 'No More Credit' in big letters.'

'He'll be feeling the pinch too. Only the pawn shop seems to be doing any business round here.'

In an hour or so Davey returned home. He'd been playing down by the river bank, the same river which once had driven the machinery for the looms before Sir John had changed over to steam.

He was filthy dirty and there was a sheepish expression on his face. He sidled into the scullery trying to avoid his mother's gaze.

'What have you been up to?' she asked suspiciously. Davey always gave himself away by the guilty expression on his face.

'Nothin', our Mam.'

'Don't you 'nothin' me,' she snapped and followed him into the scullery where he was hastily scrubbing the dirt off his face and hands.

'I didn't mean to fall in, Mam', he protested as she inspected his wet muddy clothes.

'Oh, my goodness!' she suddenly exclaimed. 'Just look at the boy's boots!'

Polly ran into the scullery to see what the damage

was as Mam held up one of Davey's scruffy feet. The boot was gaping like a huge smile where the sole had parted company with the upper. His bare toes were wiggling through the gap.

'Oh, Davey!' she said. 'They're your Sunday boots, too. Why weren't you wearing your clogs?'

"Cos they slip on the rocks,' he said lamely.

Somehow the collapse of Davey's boots was the last straw for Mam.

She sank into her rocker by the fire and tears coursed down her cheeks. She was tired and worn out with worrying about them all.

Davey crept upstairs out of the way and Polly put her arms around her mother.

'Don't cry, our Mam.'

'I'll be round the Welfare yet, you see,' she sobbed. 'I'll be at that secondhand clothes place yet, looking for charity. I never thought we'd come to this.'

'At least we've still got our beds, Mam. Mrs Hemmings will be sleeping on the floor tonight.'

'Aye. Poor woman! And she was the thrifty sort too. And now our Davey's best boots!'

Polly laid her cheek against her mother's wet, tear-stained face, remembering the fine shiny leather riding boots Francis Taylor was wearing that afternoon. Life was very unfair!

When Grace came home that evening Davey got a roasting from her too.

'When are you going to learn sense, boy?' she

shouted at him. 'We're all doing our bit to keep going and you have to be so stupid.'

'Leave him be, Grace. He's only young. Boys have to be boys,' Mam pleaded.

'Not in this house they don't,' Grace said harshly. 'He's got to grow up and be responsible. By the time I get back I expect you to be more sensible and look after our Mam. Not worry her! Understand?'

Davey hung his head.

'Get back from where?' Mam asked, dread in her voice.

'I'm going to London, Mam. Me and Chrissie Hopkins. She's got an aunty who lives at Hampstead and she reckons she can find us work in service down there. I'm going on Saturday.'

Mam looked aghast. 'But what will Pa say? You're only seventeen. You can't go gallivanting off to London at your age.'

'I can and I am, Mam. I don't much like the idea of being a servant. The hours are long and there's few days off, but I'm smart and tidy and it's better than being out of work here. I've got enough for the fare and if we get work we'll be back for our things later on. It'll be an adventure, riding on one of those new trains and all.'

'Oh, Gracie,' Mam said, throwing her arms round her elder daughter. 'What will I do without you?'

The whole family was devastated to see Grace set off to a huge place like London but no one could have been more proud than the Hopkins and the Bradshaw families as they waved their daughters off on Saturday morning.

'Eeh!' exclaimed Mrs Hopkins in her broad Lancashire dialect. 'Don't they look grand? By heck! There's no one so smart as a mill lass when she's dressed up.'

That was true. No one would have guessed that Grace and Chrissie came from homes where everyone was desperately short of money and where most of their best clothes had already gone to the pawnbroker long ago.

'Don't worry, Mam. I'll be all right,' Grace said, giving Mam a last hug. Then there were kisses all round and the girls set off to Manchester station in the vicar's little pony trap loaned specially for the occasion.

Both of the girls found work in a place called 'The Heath' and, for a little while, Polly had a bed to herself.

. . . . .

By now most of the spinning machines were idle in Coleybridge Mill. Mam was stood off along with the other women. Every morning Pa and Joseph set off with the wagon.

They had been found work breaking rocks on the moors. The younger men like Joseph were paid a shilling a ton to break the rocks while others were paid an equally miserly sum to load them into Pa's wagon. From there the load was taken into town where other mill workers hammered it into the roads. All over Lancashire the roads were being improved by the poor.

For a few months the Bradshaw family survived on the little money Pa and Joseph earned and the vegetables Polly brought home on Mondays but, bit by bit, their home was being sold to anyone prepared to give them a few shillings.

The first thing to go was the dresser.

'We can manage without it,' Mam said. 'The china can go in a box in the scullery till times get better.'

Then it was Polly's bed. Joseph took to sleeping on the bedroom floor and Polly moved in with Davey 'top to tail' fashion.

The few shillings these two items fetched bought sufficient feed for the horses without whom Pa would have no work, nor hope of improvement when times got better.

Everyone was saying what would happen 'when times got better' but there was worse to come.

CHAPTER FIVE

Winning Through

Whatever the difficulties, somehow or other the Bradshaw family managed to go to church on Sundays, but one only had to look at the way the congregation was dressed now to know that life was hard for everyone.

One autumn Sunday Polly's boots collapsed, as Davey's had done a few months earlier.

She felt very conspicuous clattering into church in her clogs. It was bad enough wearing the only dress she possessed, but to have to wear clogs all the time meant only one awful thing.

She couldn't go to see Florence.

'I'm sorry, pet,' Mam said. 'Davey will have to take a note up to the Hall.'

'But you can't say I haven't got any boots, Mam.'

'No. No. I'll just say that you are indisposed and her Ladyship will have to make of it what she likes.'

So Davey walked all the way to Denbigh Hall and handed Mam's note in at the kitchen door where

Mrs Dawkins interrogated him, in the nicest possible way. Davey, of course, didn't know the word 'indisposed'. As far as he was concerned Polly, like himself, no longer had best boots and he said so.

'That's too bad, poor love,' the plump lady said. 'Miss Florence will miss having young Polly to push her around and that. Now you just sit yourself down and Dawkins will find you a nice slice of pie and a glass of milk.'

Davey didn't want telling twice. The thought of pie put a great smile on his freckled face.

'And how's your Mam managing with the mill shut down?' she asked him as she cut the pie.

'We have to sell our things sometimes,' he said, stuffing the lovely pastry in as fast as manners would allow. 'Next week Mam says we'll have to go up to the soup kitchen and join the queue like everyone else. Pa is working with the horses carting rocks and our Joey is breaking them. It's real hard work. His hands are all blisters.'

That night the blisters finally beat Joseph.

He had been thinking of leaving the country for some time but he was loathe to forsake the family.

Now his hands were bleeding and his back ached so badly that he wondered if he'd ever walk straight again.

'I've made my mind up, Pa,' he said, as he supped the thin vegetable soup Mam had made with the things Davey had brought home from Mrs Dawkins. 'There's a ship bound for Australia in Liverpool docks right now and I aim to be on her.'

'But what about the ticket?' Mam said.

'I'll work my ticket. Ships have engines now, Mam. I'll get work in the engine-room perhaps.'

'But it's such a long way, son. How do you know you'll find work there?'

'A handbill was passed around at the Union meeting once. Land of opportunity they call it. Well, that's for me. I'll make out all right and you'll have one less mouth to feed, Mam.'

'Oh, Joey,' she said sadly. 'As if I minded that.'

'But I mind. If I get decent work I'll send money home. It's the only way for a single man with no responsibilities. There's hundreds and hundreds of miles that no one has explored yet and it's wonderful farming country, not to mention the possibility of finding gold. Imagine that, Mam!'

But Mam was not impressed.

It was hard to raise a child to manhood and then part with him forever. Australia was a very long way away and she knew as she hugged him good-bye that it was for the last time.

Joseph set off with his few belongings tied in a bundle. Mam had patched his only pair of trousers and he had spent Sunday in Pa's overalls while Mam washed the precious garments. At least he was leaving the country clean. She pressed her last two shillings into his hand.

That night the little house seemed very quiet.

When Polly kissed her goodnight Mam said,

'You're not our Polly In-between any more, my love. You're the eldest now.'

'I know,' Polly said tearfully, 'But I'd rather still be 'in-between'.'

. . . . .

It was very warm that summer and the open drains which ran the length of Notley Street stank so badly that everyone had to keep their doors and windows shut.

Flies swarmed everywhere and there was so much sickness that those who were already undernourished very soon succumbed to the fever.

The queue at the soup kitchen grew longer each day and people who had once been proud to work and support themselves now found themselves lining up for charity money.

Pa set off one morning to register for this money. Small as it was it would help out, but he came home even more despondent.

For the first time in his life he found himself unable to support his family and it was very shaming to have to queue to register for relief money. It was even worse to find that he was not entitled to any while he owned two horses.

'I might have to get rid of them,' he said to Mam, flopping into his rocker and putting his head in his hands in despair. Polly had never seen her father so worried.

'But you can't,' she said. 'I love them.' The tears were very close to the surface and her voice sounded funny. First Grace and then Joey, and now the horses. It was more than she could bear. She ran out into the yard and sat herself in the hay between the two gentle animals and cried.

Presently Pa came to find her.

'I love them too, lass,' he said, squatting beside her close to their great fluffy feet. 'I promise I won't sell them unless I absolutely have to. I shall need them again when things pick up. They're the only thing we own worth anything now.'

When Polly came home from school next afternoon the beautiful carved cradle was gone and Mam had bought a little mutton, salt, bread and coffee.

. . . . .

Florence woke that next morning with a headache.

She'd had headaches before, but never this badly. It throbbed from her eyes right over her head and down to the back of her neck and she felt very hot.

She struggled out of bed and limped with her lopsided gait across the room to the open window.

She tried to pull the heavy brocade curtains aside but all her strength had gone and she sank to her knees breathing in the cool air with her arms along the windowledge.

A housemaid found her there when she brought her breakfast tray in and ran to tell Lady Taylor's maid.

In a few minutes Florence was back in bed and her mother was sitting beside her holding a cool damp cloth to her forehead. She still wore her nightgown with the Japanese flowers on it, and her red hair hung in a thick plait instead of swathed on top of her head as it usually was.

'How pretty she looks,' Florence thought. 'Like a princess.' Then she slipped back into unconsciousness.

The doctor came and said he thought the child had meningitis and, to be honest, he was not sure if he could do very much.

'Just keep her cool,' he said and left some medicine to reduce her fever.

For three days Florence lay in a twilight world, occasionally crying out for Polly in her delirium, until at last her Ladyship sent for Mrs Dawkins.

The cook often had talks with her mistress about menus for parties and this morning she thought they would discuss a special diet for the poor sick child.

'You remember the note that came from Mrs Bradshaw, Dawkins?' her Ladyship said.

'Yes, Mi'Lady. Young Davey brought it.'

'Did he say anything about his sister's 'indisposition'? Did he say if she too was feeling unwell? I am fearful that poor Florence has contracted the meningitis from the mill children.'

'No, no, Mi'Lady. It was her shoes – or rather her lack of them.'

'Shoes?'

'Yes, Mi'Lady. She couldn't come here in clogs, Mi'Lady.'

'Good gracious, Dawkins! Do you mean my daughter lost her companion because of shoes?'

'Yes, Mi'Lady. Though it could well have been other clothing too. Folk have only what they stand up in. Everything is pawned you see.'

'You should have told me. I would have understood.'

'Maybe, Mi'Lady, but Mrs Bradshaw is a proud woman. She would have been embarrassed. It may be that she has been embarrassed enough having the carriage at her door every Monday when all her neighbours are in such a plight. Beg pardon, Mi'Lady. I'm speaking out of turn.'

Lady Taylor paced around the room. She had to do something for Florence. If Polly was well she had nothing to fear.

'Tell Hambrook I want him right away,' she said.

By the time Mr Hambrook presented himself her Ladyship was dressed in her outdoor clothes.

'I want you to take me to Notley Street,' she said.

'But, Mi'Lady, You can't. It's no place for a lady.'

'Our workers live there, don't they?'

'Yes, Mi'Lady, but it smells and you won't like it.'

'Like it or not I want to see Mrs Bradshaw, so no more 'buts'. My daughter's life may depend on it.'

Without further ado they set off, with Mr Hambrook wishing with all his heart that her Ladyship would change her mind.

The carriage turned into Notley Street by Shawcross's shop corner, where ragged children clustered on the step waiting for a handout like small beggars.

At open doorways women stood dejectedly clutching their pale sickly babies while toddlers held onto their mothers' tattered skirts, with their fingers stuffed into their mouths to stave off the hunger.

Their sad eyes followed the bright shiny carriage with its sleek grey pony and the elegant lady.

At one house a woman with wild straggly hair and an even wilder expression called out, 'What have you come for, Missus? Come to gloat have you?'

Another woman took up the cry. 'Go back to your fine house on t'hill. You've no business here gawping at us when we're starving.'

'Do you want to go back, Mi'Lady?' Mr Hambrook asked anxiously. Lady Taylor squared her shoulders.

'Of course not. Please continue to the Bradshaw house.'

'The smell gets worse down this end, Mi'Lady. Due to the drains running downhill and having nowhere proper to go.'

Her Ladyship took a small hankie from her reticule, but that was the only sign she made that the stench was so offensive.

Davey reached 135 before the carriage did.

He'd seen it turn the top corner and he had run all the way down the back alley and clambered over the yard wall.

'Mam! Mam! Mr Hambrook is comin' and he's got her Ladyship an' all,' he shouted breathlessly, tumbling into the scullery.

'Oh my goodness!' Mam exclaimed. 'She's not coming here is she?'

She cast an anxious glance around her bare home. All that remained was the table and its four plain chairs. Bit by bit everything had gone, even the beautiful carved cradle, and only yesterday the rockers had gone too.

She gathered up Daisy and hastily washed her face. She had never been so ashamed of their poor threadbare clothing and worn-out clogs.

'She's stoppin' here, our Mam,' Davey whispered peeping over the top of the windowledge. 'Shall I open the door?'

'No. You stay put and behave,' she said sharply, then she went to the door, holding Daisy on her hip with one hand while she straightened her hair with the other.

Mr Hambrook stood on the door step.

'Her Ladyship would like a word, Ma'am,' he said.

'Tell her Ladyship she's welcome if she cares to step down,' Mam said.

The wealthy mill-owner's wife met the carter's wife on the doorstep; the one beautifully dressed with her shining copper hair topped by a jaunty green straw hat with a feather, the other old before her time, dressed in a drab grey skirt and a cotton shirt with the sleeves rolled up above her skinny elbows. Her once -luxuriant brown hair was tinged with grey and it was scraped back in a knot.

'Mi'Lady,' Mam said, making a stilted little curtsey. 'Will you come in away from the dreadful smell?'

'Thank you, Mrs Bradshaw,' her Ladyship said, and to the amazement of all the neighbours she entered the Bradshaws' bare livingroom.

'How can I help you, Mi'Lady? Polly is at school this afternoon.' She pulled a chair from under the table and quickly dusted it with her apron. Lady Taylor sat down.

'It's about Polly that I came, Mrs Bradshaw. I know there is some difficulty about her footwear, but my daughter is very poorly and asks for her friend constantly. Will you let her come tomorrow? I fear Florence may die of the fever if we do not give her something to live for. Please, I beg you!'

'Who told you about the shoes, Mi'Lady?'

Lady Taylor's eyes fell on Davey, peeping round Mam's bed curtain. His expression was one of fear lest Mam gave him a roasting again.

'I don't know, Mrs Bradshaw, but it's of no consequence. I have brought a couple of pairs of boots with me and a few things you might find useful. Please do say that Polly can come. She is such a good friend to Florence.'

Davey breathed a sigh of relief.

If Mam had had the time to reflect on this conversation she might have been amused that the tables were turned about and that it was her Ladyship who was doing the begging now.

'Very well, Mi'Lady. Tomorrow then. And we thank you for the shoes and things. I cannot deny that they are very welcome. I'm only sorry that I cannot offer you some refreshment. In better times maybe.'

'We all pray for that I can assure you,' her Ladyship said and, with that, the carriage hurried homewards to the fine house on the edge of the moor.

Mr Hambrook picked Polly up next morning.

Her dress was mended but she wore a white pinafore and a pair of plain housemaid's shoes that Lady Taylor had brought.

As the carriage went up the street it was followed by dozens of pairs of eyes.

'There goes Polly Bradshaw grown into a fine lady,' a boy shouted, but Polly looked straight ahead and ignored the cat calls.

Florence was very ill indeed.

She lay in her huge bed with the crisp white linen and the flowered counterpane and she didn't seem to know anyone.

Polly decided to treat the situation as though Florence knew and understood every word she said.

'We've been doing Australia today, Florence. Our Joseph has gone to Australia you know. There's lots and lots of land there for farming they say, and gold and opals. Wouldn't it be fine if our Joey could find gold? Then we'd be rich and I could buy back the cradle from Lawry Mark's pawnshop.'

She sat by the bed and wiped Florence's brow, and all the time she talked and talked.

She told Florence about the soup kitchen and the Relief Committee who gave out money and clothing to the folk who were starving.

'And did you hear about what happened to Billy Jenkins? Someone reported him for claiming for five children when everyone knows their Charlie died two weeks ago. And you should see your mill now. Down in the sorting shed they've set up a school for grownups. Can you imagine that? The men are doing sums and writing and learning their ABCs and the women are doing sewing.'

Polly spent two days sitting with Florence and each evening Mr Hambrook took her home. Daisy was sick again and Mam was distraught because she had no money for medicines. The little house reeked of tar steaming in a pot on the stove. Polly told the unconscious Florence about this as she sat mopping her friend's brow on the fourth morning. 'We came up here from the country and we've had nought but trouble since. Half our family are gone and now Daisy is real poorly. Mam looks so old and Pa is going to have to sell the horses. I don't want them to go, Florence. They're like my family.'

Tears choked her throat at this point, but she went on. 'I wonder what you'd hate to lose most in the world. All right, I know you've got a funny foot, but the rest of you is pretty.'

Lady Taylor had just crept into the room in time to hear most of Polly's chattering.

'Here,' she said, almost in a whisper. 'Have some milk and some of Mrs Dawkin's cookies. You must be getting tired, Polly. I'll leave them here on the table. I'll be in my room if you need me.'

Polly thanked her and took the milk. She had hated milk on the farm but now it seemed the nicest thing she had ever tasted. She sat by the window and looked out over the park. How peaceful and green it was – a far cry from Notley Street.

Suddenly there was a murmur from the bed.

'Polly,' Florence said in a whisper.

Polly was immediately on her feet and across the room.

'I'm here! I'm here!' she cried and tears of relief welled up in her eyes.

Forgetting her place entirely she ran to the door and shouted,

'Mi'Lady! Mi'Lady! She's awake!' then she ran back to the bed where Florence was trying to sit up.

'Don't move, Florence,' she said. 'You've been very ill. Lie still and I'll put some pillows around you.'

Florence's Mama and two housemaids came running in, then his Lordship without his jacket. No one had ever seen Sir John in his braces before.

Everyone was overjoyed to see that the fever had broken at last and that Florence seemed so much better. She was holding Polly's hand and she was smiling.

'I'm so glad you came again,' she said softly.

That evening when Polly was about to leave Sir John followed her out into the stableyard where Mr Hambrook waited with the pony.

'I hope you'll come again, Polly,' he said. 'I knew my first instincts about you were true. You are a real friend to my daughter and I wish there was more I could do to show my appreciation. My wife tells me things need doing in Notley Street. I'll have to see what can be done, eh?'

'Yes, sir. Thank you, sir.'

'Thank you, Polly.'

He passed up a bag of goodies for her to take home, not knowing that Mrs Dawkins had already placed one under the seat as usual.

Polly said goodbye and promised she would come again.

Two days later a gang of men began digging a

drain down the middle of the back alley in Notley Street and Sir John's agent called to ask Pa if his horses were capable of towing barges.

'My Belle and Moppet can do anything. Anything!' Pa declared proudly.

'Then present yourself at the canal jetty tomorrow with one horse and we'll see if you can tow a barge of Indian cotton. A big consignment has arrived at last.'

Pa was speechless. One horse at a time! That would mean one could be resting on alternate days. Indian cotton! Not the best by any means, but the spinners and weavers could start again.

They would have a wage at last.

He picked Daisy up and threw her over his shoulder.

'I've got a feeling my Polly In-between had something to do with this,' he said munching his way through a huge piece of Mrs Dawkin's veal and ham pie.

'I don't know how,' said Polly.

'When I was at school there were three words I learned of Latin. They were in a history book about the Romans and they were *veni, vidi, vici*. They mean 'I came, I saw, I conquered'. I've never forgotten them though I've never had a use for them before. I think they were written for you, my lass.'

'Oh, Pa,' Polly said, smiling broadly. 'Latin is no use to me. I like Geography best. And as for the conquering bit, well, what have I ever conquered?'

'We've all been fighting battles lately, In-between, and there's probably still a few ahead, but we'll win through, just like you did with Miss Florence. Yes, my lass. I think we've actually turned the corner. What do you think, Davey boy?'

Davey looked up from the hearth where he'd just captured a cockroach.

'I don't want to learn Latin, Pa,' he said emphatically. 'I haven't learned my seven times table yet.'

For the first time for months the little house rang with laughter.

PLACES TO VISIT

1. *Helmshore Textile Museum and Higher Mill Museum*
   situated one mile south of Haslingden, Lancs.
   Two original cotton mills, now open to the public.

2. *The Lewis Museum of Textile Machinery*
   Blackburn, Lancs.

3. *Towneley Hall*
   Mansion with displays showing how people lived, their
   furnishings and artefacts etc. 1½ miles south of
   Burnley, Lancs.

4. *The Weavers Triangle, Burnley*
   A triangle between the Leeds and Liverpool Canals where
   mills and factories still line the canal. Concerned with the
   transport of cotton.

5. *Crich Transport Museum*
   Near Chatsworth in Derbyshire.

6. *The Victoria and Albert Museum, London*
   for clothing and artefacts.

7. *The Science Museum, Exhibition Rd, London*
   for machinery and transport.